# This book belongs to…

_____

_____

# Pronunciation Guide

Chhoti – Chh-o-tee

Chintu – Chin-too

Dahan – Duh-hun

Didi – Dee-dee

Gujia – Goo-jee-yaa

Gulaal – Goo-laal

Hola Mohalla – Holaa-mohullaa

Holi – Ho-lee

Holi Hai – Ho-lee Hay

Holika – Ho-lee-kaa

Holi Milan – Ho-lee Mee- lun

Pichkari – Pitch-kaa-ree

Prahlad – Pruh-laad

Thabal Chongba – Thu-Baal Chong-Baa

Thandai – Thun-da-yee

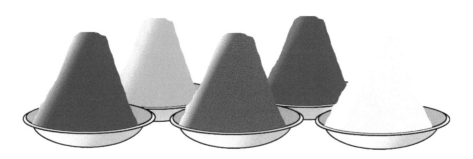

*Note for parents: Our books provide a glimpse into the beautiful cultural diversity of India, including occasional mythology references. Given India's size and diversity, Holi is celebrated in a multitude of different ways. In this book, we showcase elements of Holi celebration that are best suited for young readers to follow.*

Maya & Neel's India Adventure Series, Book 3

# Let's Celebrate Holi!

## India's Festival of Colors

Raise Multicultural Kids

Written by:
Ajanta & Vivek

Edited by:
Janelle Diller

This is a map of India. India is a big country. It has many states, languages, festivals, and dances.

Holi is one of the most fun festivals of India. It's called the Festival of Colors. It's celebrated all over India in many different ways.

Maya, Neel and Chintu meet their cousin Ameya in India. A sister or girl cousin in India is called *Didi*. Ameya lives in a big city with tall buildings.

"I am very excited that you came to visit me," Ameya says. "Holi starts tomorrow. You're going to love this holiday!"

"We love every Indian holiday!" Neel says. "Tell us about Holi, *Didi*."

# The story of Holi

Once upon a time, an evil king ruled in India. He thought he was the most powerful king of the world. He wanted everyone to pray to him.

A brave little boy named *Prahlad* wasn't afraid though. He refused to pray to the evil king.

The king tried to scare *Prahlad* with mean words. But it did not work. *Prahlad* still refused to pray to him. The king got very angry. He thought of a way to hurt *Prahlad*.

The king's sister, *Holika,* had a magical power. She could sit in fire without getting hurt.

# The story of Holi (cont.)

The king made *Prahlad* sit on *Holika's* lap in the fire. The king thought the fire would hurt *Prahlad* but not *Holika*.

But when they sat in the fire, a magical thing happened. The fire did not hurt *Prahlad* at all. Instead, *Holika* disappeared in the fire!

Because *Prahlad* was such a nice boy, the evil king and his sister could not hurt him at all. We celebrate Holi to show that good always wins over evil.

A long time ago, people celebrated Holi by burning a bonfire. They put burned wood or ash on their foreheads. Later on, they started using colored powder instead of ash to make it more fun.

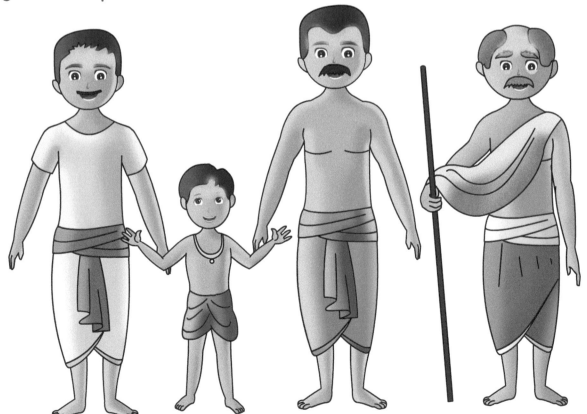

The kids walk into Ameya's house. They notice beautiful flowers all around. "Holi is celebrated during the Spring season. This is when many flowers bloom" Ameya explains.

Next, Ameya gives them some white clothes. "Holi is played with bright colors. So the whiter your clothes are, the more colors you can get on them".

Maya and Neel look worried. "But we didn't bring any colors to play Holi with," Maya says.

"Don't worry, we are going to the market right now. We will buy lots of Holi colors" Ameya says.

Maya and Neel have never seen a more colorful market. They see heaps of colored powder – red, blue, pink, green, yellow, purple.

"This colored powder is called *gulaal*. We put it on each other's face," Ameya explains.

Neel picks up something that looks like a water gun.

"What are those, *Didi*?" he asks. "Oh, this is a *pichkari*. You fill it with colored water and spray it on each other," Ameya replies.

"We also fill balloons with water and throw them at each other," Ameya says. "Like these?" Maya asks. "Yes, like those," Ameya smiles.

The kids clap their hands and laugh. "Just think of all the fun!"

In the evening, neighbors light a bonfire. It burns brightly. The kids join everyone in the neighborhood.

"What are they doing, *Didi*?" Neel asks.

"Today is the night before Holi. We call today *Chhoti* Holi or Mini Holi. Remember how *Holika* disappeared in the fire? This fire is a symbol of that story. So we call the burning of the bonfire *Holika Dahan*."

The next morning the kids wake up very excited. Today is Holi!

They start preparing for the day.

Ameya says "Let's bring our *pichkaris* and water balloons in the bathroom. Then we won't spill any color in the house."

Ameya mixes the colored powder in the big buckets. The kids then fill up the water balloons and *pichkaris* with the colored water. They are now ready for Holi!

They put on their white Holi clothes and step outside.

Maya and Neel don't know the other kids. So the four of them play Holi with each other.

They splash red, yellow, blue, pink, green, and purple colors on each other.

"Splash!" Suddenly someone dumps a bucket full of colored water on Neel's head and shouts, "Holi Hai! Today is Holi."

Maya and Ameya laugh till their sides hurt.

"Everyone is your friend on the day of Holi," Ameya says. "So let's play with all the other kids."

Maya, Neel and even Chintu join all the kids, spraying water and saying, "Holi Hai!"

Soon a man with a *Dhol*, an Indian drum, shows up.

Everyone sings and dances with the drums. They leap and shout and laugh.

The kids play Holi all afternoon.

Then they go home and scrub, scrub, scrub off the colors. Chintu scrubs, scrubs, scrubs, too.

Finally, Ameya pulls out a giant book and reads to them about the festival. "Different places in India celebrate Holi in their own special way," she says.

**INFO ZOOM** — Holi around India

In the city of **Ahmedabad (State of Gujarat)**, they hang a buttermilk pot high up in the air. Boys climb on top of each other to reach it while girls playfully throw colored water on them. The boy who reaches the top and breaks the pot is declared the Holi King!

In the state of Manipur, they do a special dance called *Thabal Chongba*. This means "Moonlight Dance". People hold hands and dance in big circles.

# Holi around India (cont.)

In the state of **Punjab**, they celebrate with an event called *Hola Mohalla* to show how strong they are. They stand on running horses or spin massive rings while balancing on sticks.

After the story time, the children change into beautiful Indian clothes. Ameya takes Neel and Maya to the kitchen for some snacks and drinks.

"*Didi*, what is this white drink?" Maya asks.

"This is called *Thandai*. Think of it as Indian milkshake. People drink it on the day of Holi". The kids take a long sip. It is sweet, milky and cold.

"Yum!" Chintu squeaks.

Neel spots half-moon shaped snacks. "This looks yummy, too. What is it, *Didi*?"

"These are called *Gujia*. They are crunchy, sweet dumplings. This is another famous Holi snack of India." The kids munch on a plate full of *Gujia*. They wash them down with more *Thandai*.

"And now it's time for *Holi Milan*. This is when neighbors visit each other's home and exchange plate full of sweets," Ameya says.

They take a plate full of *Gujia* to their neighbor's house. She greets them with a big smile and warm hugs.

She invites them in and offers more snacks and *Thandai.*

"Do you see the giant, beautiful moon today, kids?" the neighbor asks.

The moonlight fills up the whole room. "Holi is always celebrated on a full moon day when the moon is biggest and roundest," she explains.

The kids lean over the balcony to take a better look at the moon. It is almost like the moon is celebrating Holi along with them.

"We had so much fun today. Holi is one of our favorite festivals now", Neel says.

"We can't wait for our next adventure. We wonder where that will be. We hope you can join us then," Maya, Neel and Chintu say.

"Until then, Namaste!"

# Let's look back on our wonderful Holi Celebration...

What is Holi?
(India's festival of colors)

What did the evil king want everyone to do?
(Pray to him)

What is the burning of the bonfire called?
(Holika Dahan)

Why did Prahlad not get hurt but Holika did?
(Because Prahlad was nice & Holika was evil)

What is the colored powder called? (Gulaal)

What is the water gun called? (Pichkari)

Holi is celebrated when the moon is...?
(Biggest and Roundest)

What food and drink do people have during Holi?
(Gujia and Thandai)

# My Holi Story

_____

_____

_____

_____

_____

_____

_____

_____

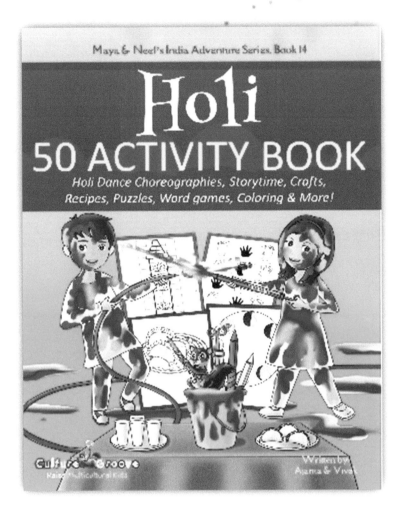

# About the Authors

**Ajanta Chakraborty** was born in Bhopal, India, and moved to North America in 2001. She earned an MS in Computer Science from the University of British Columbia and also earned a Senior Diploma in Bharatanatyam, a classical Indian dance, to feed her spirit.

Ajanta quit her corporate consulting job in 2011 and took the plunge to run Bollywood Groove (and also Culture Groove) full-time. The best part of her work day includes grooving with classes of children as they leap and swing and twirl to a Bollywood beat.

**Vivek Kumar** was born in Mumbai, India, and moved to the US in 1998. Vivek has an MS in Electrical Engineering from The University of Texas, Austin, and an MBA from the Kellogg School of Management, Northwestern University.

Vivek has a very serious day job in management consulting. But he'd love to spend his days leaping and swinging, too.

---

We have been featured on:

---

We are independent authors who want to help **Raise Multicultural Kids**! We rely on your support to sustain our work:

✓ Drop us an Amazon review at: **CultureGroove.com/books**

✓ **Share our books as Gifts & Party Favors** (bulk order discounts)

✓ Schedule our unique **'Dancing Bookworms' Virtual Author Visits**

✓ Join our **FREE** Monthly Stories & Dances workshops: **CultureGroove.com/FREE**

**Many thanks!**

Culture Groove
Raise Multicultural Kids